A FLASH OF SILVER

A FLASH OF SILVER

A JONO GREY SHORT STORY

DAVID GEARING

AKUSAI PUBLISHING

A FLASH OF SILVER
A JONO GREY SHORT STORY

There was this one time when I was fifteen when there were ghosts everywhere," I tell the bartender as she pours an extra shot for me. Her name is, well, I forget, but she's newish here and already knows that I'm full of shit.

"You always drink two shots at a time?" she asks.

"It's for my friend. Name's Rusty. He'll be meeting me soon."

She rolls her eyes, but with a coy smile.

I think she'll fit in fine. This is the type of place that gets its clientele from the airports. People coming in and figuring out they might as well drink all of the airsickness away. Or, if they're like me, come in and get drunk before the flight. Take the edge off the take-off and landings.

This is the type of bar that seems to only have the jukebox playing classic rock because no one else can figure out how to get in and change the records.

And yes, thank the gods, they still use records.

I could fix it with just a flick of my finger, but no one has asked. And my usual bartender, Sandra, seems to be missing these last few days. I'm not the type to ask where she is, seeing as how it's none of my business.

But that doesn't mean I don't want to ask. I am human, after all.

Well, mostly human.

This place's electricity bill goes to the powering of all the buzzing neon signs around the place. Because of the pinks and blues and yellows, I don't know the color of this alcohol anymore. I just know it tastes like whiskey but might be flavored with cherry or something.

Or maybe I'm buzzing and I'm tasting what I want. Or she just poured in cherry juice in here and I haven't noticed.

At least it's not Visine.

I hold out the glass to what's her name and say, "I lived in a small house while my parents hurled toasters at each other clear across the country. My aunts and uncles called my mom names behind my back, but the ghosts, well, they told me everything. Not a lot you can keep from the tired and nosy spirits that walk amongst us."

She nods at me again, not really paying attention. But she pushes her blond hair to one side and leans over onto the bar, resting on her elbows. Her hazel eyes narrow, then she leans in and says, "What are you going on about, old man?"

I'll ignore that, instead saying, "Although to be fair, it was a small house that had to have been a hundred years old inside, but looked maybe thirty or forty years old outside. The soft brown panels on the outside of the house were installed by my grandfather. Wide windows, two stories. The house had a look that said, 'Come inside and enjoy a cup of coffee'."

"My grandparents have that kind of a house," she says. "In some suburb of Tucson or something. You know old people."

"Old?" I ask. She stands up and nods. Her chest stays in one place, even as she jerks upward and pushes along the glasses on the bar.

"Yeah. My parents had me old."

"Like how old?"

"They're retired."

"That doesn't mean anything, honey. People these days, they retire early after hitting it big."

"Didn't I say we lived in Tucson? You're only rich," she says using finger quotes, "if you lived in the Cat Foothills. And even then, you were USA average."

"Damn," I say.

"Yup."

"You believe in haunted houses?"

She shakes her head. "Nope. I saw all that shit on TV. Don't believe a damned part of it."

I wave a single finger and watch as a flame pulls itself out of the wall. Her eyes lock with mine and she says, "Trick of mirrors." She blows some of her bangs up and away from her eyes, then turns her head away from me. "Good try, though."

The fire burns a bright blue and then extinguishes into the air. The smell of smoke wafts through the air, waving from a thin gray trail to thin air. The fizzling sound only slightly catches her ear.

"Well, let me tell you about this house, then? Tell you what. You don't believe me, I'll pay you two hundred percent tip and I walk out of here."

"And if you win?" she says. She tucks her hands into her pockets.

"You don't owe me anything."

She relaxes.

"Just free drinks."

She rolls those hazelnut eyes and says, "Sure sure. Whatever."

———

LIKE I SAID, the house looked new outside. When you get inside, though, you walked into a thick, dark carpet that snagged against your shoes. Everything was a dark, wooden paneling that just made the dark, cold winters feel even more bleak than they already were.

I'm talking about the kind of setting that makes you understand why people sought the soothing release of death.

And the creaks. My gods! Did everything creak.

And I mean everything.

The inside always smelled like coffee the way gas stations always smelled like car exhaust and bars always smell like smoke.

Dear lords, this had to have been nearly eighty years ago. Where did the time go?

"WAIT," she says, suddenly not moving any further than five feet from me. "How old?"

"Eighty years?" I say.

She leans over and seems to be analyzing my face.

"What are you looking for?" I'm stoic, staring her right in the eyes. Asserting dominance.

"The scars. From the surgery."

"Honey, this is no surgery. This is pure magic."

"Fine. Keep your secrets," she says.

"Can I continue now?"

She waves me on.

SO LIKE I SAID, it must have been about eighty years since that time. The house is long abandoned, lived in by one of my cousin's cousins or something like that. I don't know. I won't step foot in that town again after they pretty much ran me out of town. You save a town from an imp and somehow you're the bad guy.

I remembered one morning while I sat in a wooden chair, the wood still cold against my bare legs, and I held a ceramic bowl of cereal and milk and listening to the radio. Some shadow hero stopping crime sprees all across the country. Riveting stuff. Really.

But just as a commercial came on, there was something moving on the wooden desk next to me. It was one of those drawing desks, with the rolling covers that came down to cover the pens and papers and stuff.

Except there was something spinning the wooden handle. Round and round.

My eyes got big, my heart jumped in my throat. But all I could do was watch.

It spun around. Then around again. Slowly. Mocking me.

I stopped eating. I stopped listening. Just transfixed.

"G-grandma," I tried to say. I'm not sure what came out of my mouth at that moment, but my grandmother came in anyway.

"What are you going on about?"

I pointed at the desk, my little finger trembling.

"What?" Grandma put her hand on the desk, rubbing it back and forth like she was petting it. "I don't see anything." My grandmother was a tough old broad. Big curly white hair and soft milky white skin that no one else in my family ever got. She was a porcelain doll, that woman, with rosy cheeks and a big smile and bigger nose.

"There was something moving that."

"Moving what?" she looked at the door. Then at me, like I was the crazy one.

"The handle. Spinning."

"It's just Herman," she said. "He's harmless." She turned and walk back to the kitchen, wiping her hands on a red and white checkered towel she used to dry dishes. "Don't bother him, Herman. You're scaring the boy."

And that was that. She walked back into the room and that was it.

"YOU'RE terrible at telling ghost stories," the waitress says. She hasn't moved away from me. At the end of the bar, a trucker, probably a new trucker based on the baby size of his beard, sat and seemed more interested in me than the waitress. He took off his black leather jacket, revealing a wife-beater and broad, dark skinned shoulders. Clearly worked out when he had the time.

"I'm not telling you a ghost story. I'm telling you about my grandma's haunted house."

"You're full of shit," she says. The waitress, what's-her-name, she pours me another drink into my shot glass and says, "If your story doesn't pick up soon, this'll cost ya seven bucks."

"That's an expensive shot." I eyeball it. "I don't even see gold flakes or anything else."

"That's an asshole tax. You're boring me," she says.

Yes, she'll do fine here for sure.

• • •

AS I WAS SAYING, that was my first introduction to Herman.

That night, my grandmother sends me to bed. I get the bedroom that is the smallest, has barely enough room for a twin bed and a dresser and a nightstand. That's about it. Even the closet was about as wide as a door. And a horrible floral pattern. Bright pink and mint green on a god awful eggshell white background. Made you fucking gag.

God I'm glad this century has some fucking taste.

Okay, okay, I see I'm losing you. So that night, I'm on the bed, watching as the moon shines through the vertical blinds on the tiny window. The silver disc is about as bright as electric light you'd see on the street. Lit up the sky. And I'm watching it because I've always been drawn to the night, you know? Drawn to it flies to shit.

And I hear a creak coming from the hallway.

I figure it's my grandma, going to bed. My grandpa had been dead about three months at that point, and it was just me and her. Sometimes my aunt when she wasn't staying at her boyfriends.

And yes, I knew she was staying at her beau's.

So I'm here, listening to creaking floorboards in a shining pale moonlight. It's not exactly restful. Or romantic.

I sit up, feeling my shoulders just get goosebumps from how cold it is there. Did I mention it was Wisconsin? Fucking freezing up there. So I'm there freezing and waiting for the creaking to stop, but it won't.

I get up, listening to the door.

It cracks open. Which is weird because it swung into the room. Not out into the door.

I take a step back, thinking my grandma is coming in. Me in my shorts and nothing else, the carpet does nothing to soothe my feet at all. I could jump and hit my head on the short ceiling at any moment. The moon somehow gives the entire room a baby blue glow, you know. The color of static electricity. And I'm waiting for the door to finish opening, but nothing happens.

I don't know why I did it, but I stay there asking, "Grandma?"

And nothing.

My finger grips the handle, on the inside, you know. So the ghost doesn't just grab my fingers. Last thing you want is a cold touch on your fingertips. Especially when you can't see what it's from.

Counting to three, my hand pulls back, my elbow damn near hits the closet door. Then there's no one there in the black hallway. Like pitch black. Nothing. The hallway is a measly twenty feet, if that. You go from room to room to room and I swear there's nothing there.

Absolutely fucking nothing.

I'm standing there and looking side to side.

"Grandma?" I ask. And sure, I guess I expected an answer, but I kinda didn't want one. Cuz whatever voice I would have gotten, I was sure it wouldn't be my grandmother's.

My closet door opens wide, swift enough to blow air right past my shoulders. So I do what a fifteen fucking boy does. I yelped like a little girl--sorry, I know, it's not very p.c. of me, but it was what it was--and I jumped into the hallway.

The bedroom door closes on me. Just closes. Which is a feat because the carpet was so thick that you can't help but struggle to move that light weight door. The dragging sound was loud, you know.

So things are moving, and that's great.

But the creepy thing is the dark breathing. Like heavy and dark. It's everywhere. Behind me, next to me, down the hallway. Everywhere.

So I start talking to the ghost, right? I figure, he's watching me. Doing this shit. Assert dominance, right?

"Herman?" I ask. "What are you doing?" But I'm whispering, because let's be honest. I'm a fifteen-year-old boy at this point, talking to a figment of my imagination. I mean, I believed in ghosts because of--reasons. That's a story for a whole other time.

But there's this ghost breathing everywhere.

Like everywhere. I even feel the warmth. On my neck, on my ear. Against the back of my arms. My feet. Coming from the walls.

Everything feels warm as hot breath.

And I walk toward my grandma's bedroom. Because you want to know. Am I just hearing shit or is someone else hearing it? Misery, right? That bitch just loves company.

So I'm walking the three feet to my grandma's door. I open it slowly.

And my grandma is on her bed. Her arms are spread out to her side, the bedspread pulled back to just above her ass. Her back is bare, and as much as you don't wanna see your grandma that way, you don't want to see the silver flashes, like fuzzy light, just above her back.

It's one of those things, you know, looking through the corner of your eyes and you think, maybe there's something there, but you look straight on and you can't see it.

THE WAITRESS practically sits on the bar, looking at me with both eyes wide open. Hazelnuts staring right into my soul--if I still had one. She pushes her blond hair over, tilting her head like a cocker spaniel. "You're shitting me."

"Nope," I say. "I've seen some shit." A shot and the ceremonial knocking two times of the shot glass against the bar. "Let me tell you."

"I'm still not sure I believe a word coming out of your lying ass mouth, but I'm intrigued," she says. "Here." She fills my first shot glass. The second one still sits in front of me.

Waiting for Rusty.

"Where is your friend, anyway?" she asks. "This shot is dying here."

"Not as fast as my grandma that night," I say.

Her eyes fucking get as wide as wide can be. The old adage that my mom use to day was "wide as saucers," but really who says saucers anymore? They were wide as the moon that night. The same night my grandmother was about to die from some spectral silver glint in the air.

"So the silver glint," I say to the waitress, "hovers over her back. My grandma isn't asleep. She's not awake either. Like in some sort of coma. Her mouth was agape and I swear her eyes were sort of slightly open.

"I pointed at my grandmother and tried to focus on the silver glint, but I couldn't get a good look at it, you know? No matter how I tried to look at it, it just wouldn't focus."

"Then what?" she asked.

I smile. I had her right where I wanted her.

. . .

SO I EASED on over toward the bed. What's gross is, even though I knew there was some creepy shit going on, I can still my sideboob of my grandma's tits just pressed against the bed. Saggy but surprisingly smooth skin just popping out of her side and as much as I want to push that image out of my mind, it pales in comparison to the silvery glint lowering slowly and slowly over her back.

I pulled my hand to it, trying to take it out of the thin air.

But I kept feeling something cold. Something that was keeping that silvery light knife or whatever it was in the air. I grabbed at it again.

By this time, I'm crying. Salty tears hugging my cheeks and falling onto my bare toes and making dark stains on the bed sheets.

"Grandma," I say. "Wake up." Grabbing at her legs, I pull and push and pull and push and hope that she'll wake up. Her body waddles but nothing happens.

I SWEAR AT THIS POINT, the waitress hasn't paid attention to anyone else in the bar. The other patrons who haven't been listening in, they just give up and wander out of the bar. "Fuck this" and "Terrible service." You know how assholes are.

Then I say loud and deep, "Shhh."

The waitress jumps back and rattles the bottles behind her. The dark wood shelf shakes. Even the glasses shudder at my story.

"Stop that," she says.

I smirk. "Why? That's what it said."

"What said?"

"Herman."

"Bullshit."

I shake my head. "I wish." I take the next shot and watch the room as the eyes all look at me. Waiting, searching for the rest of the story. I snap my finger and the man next to me, a tall guy with a dark heavy beard and light brown jacket with one of those lamb's wool linings twitches.

He even wheezes as he tries to catch his breath.

There's a sliver of silver light that flashes for just a moment, literally lightning quick just above the bartender. The other patrons at the bar collectively hold their breaths.

A snort and a chuckle carries through the air to my ears. But no one else seems to hear it except for me.

Still, I continue.

"My hand grabs at the silver ghost knife in the air and I'm wrapping my hand around something that's so cold I swear I'm getting frostbite." I shift in my seat.

There's one shot left in front of me, and if Rusty doesn't get his ass down here soon, it's going in my stomach instead of his.

"And I'm grunting and pulling, my feet clinging to the bed and I'm trying to pull something. And I'm swearing at this ghost. Saying, 'Fuck you, Herman. Go to hell'." And I pause, looking around the room. "And then something happens."

"What?" the waitress mutters, barely a whisper.

"What happens is there's a flicker of something. If you could really see a shadow in the darkness, I guess that's what it was. Flashing and flickering. So I said it again. 'Go to hell. Go to Hell, Herman.' And it starts to work, I guess. The ghostly knife starts to fade and flicker like a bulb that's about to go out. I can hear the breathing and the groaning. Herman, I guess."

"Why was Herman trying to kill her?"

"I didn't find out until later," I tell them. "But he was upset that my Grandmother had invited me into the house. He couldn't touch me. You can't kill what doesn't have a soul. But she did. And that was the best way to get to me."

"Wait, you don't have a soul?" the man next to me says. His fleece jacket, I notice, starts to droop off his shoulder. He's so into my story that he can't keep himself together.

"It's a figure of speech," I say and shrug it off, literally.

Except, you know, when it's not.

"So anyway," I say, "the knife starts to flicker. So I shout it louder at where I assume Herman's head is. I shout at him, 'Go to Hell.'" I shout that last part so loud that everyone moves about six inches away from me. The waitress gasps and grabs for her chest.

"Jesus Christ," she says.

"Jesus has nothing to do with this, ma'am. The ghost--Herman--he took a step backward. The only way I knew that was because the wall started to shake. Something fell against it. The breathing got heavier, and louder. Somehow I felt it on my skin and inside of me. But he's breathing. So I shouted it again.

"Go to Hell.

"Go to Hell.

"And before long, there's a fizzling sound in the air. Like listening to a soft drink just after you shake it up and pop it open. The fuzzing and crackling of something. A smell of fire and burning stones and charcoal. But everything grows cold. The shadow's outline just flashes like a thin gray line around a human-like shape."

Rusty comes down the three steps that separates the bar from the pinball machines and one pool table on the far northern end of the long but narrow building. He shakes his head, knowing damn well what I'm doing. His rust-colored beard--the reason why his nickname is Rusty, though he hates when I call him that--is finely combed this time.

That's what's been taking him.

"You're so stupid," he mutters and sits next to me.

"The outline flickers, and as much as I try to look at it directly, like the knife, I just can't see it. I can't see any of it. But I do see one thing clearly."

"Your grandmother?" the waitress asks.

I shake my head slowly. I peer upwards, nudging Rusty. He does the fastest nod in the world and downs the shot next to me.

"Nope," I say. "The knife. The silver light that had this ghostly glint in the air, it was a real knife all of a sudden. I had to dive across the bed just to stop it from falling down into my grandmother's back. I never scrambled so hard before in my life. And barefoot in a thick carpet that felt like it was trying to grab my toes to keep me still. So there I am watching as this freezing wind just takes over the room, but the shadowy figure is gone. Herman is disappeared somewhere. Somehow.

"But I have to stop that knife. I reach out, thinking I'll stop it but I can't get a grip for it.

"The carpet lets go of me, like it was listening to me. And I'm jumping across the bed. Diving across it. The knife barely scrapes my forearm, but I have it tucked away in my hands. But my dumbass, I'm hitting the wall on the other end with my head and shoulder. Damn near knock myself out but my grandma is safe from the knife."

Rusty is trying to hide his laughter. He taps the shot glass on the bar, hoping to get someone's attention.

No one even budges. "Fine," he mutters. "Fuck 'em." He gets up and starts sliding through the swing door to back behind the bar.

"And would you know, the only thing that I hear after that is my grandmother snorting and struggling to pull herself around. Her sagging tits are barely covered by the sheets that she doesn't bother to use to cover herself. I can't look, but it's like a car wreck you know. Even at fifteen, gay as hell. They're there, so you're gonna look."

Rusty pours himself some whiskey. Blue label. He shakes his head, chuckling. "Yer a sick fuck."

"And my grandma looks at me and she tells me to get out of the room and why am I holding a knife in her bedroom. She tells me that we'll talk about it in the morning. Except we never did."

The waitress stands up tall, her eyes narrow. "And that's it? Nothing happened?"

"No one died, and my grandmother lived for a whole other six months before she died from a fall."

Rusty decides that we need to hear his voice. "Jesus. At least the ghost woulda killed 'er in 'er sleep."

"Well, I saved her and got rid of the ghost that haunted that house," I say. "Or at least I think I did."

"What do you mean?"

"Every once in a while, I feel like I still see the silver glint in the air. Like a fuzzy light just outside of my field of vision."

There's a thin dot of reflected light that falls to the wall behind the waitress. It travels down, slowly, just over the bottles of booze until it falls onto the waitress's shoulder. Then it moves to her head, up to her eyes. She shakes her head, rubs her eyes.

Then the swooshing sound of metal and wooden in the air.

A knife falls down from the air--thin air as the others will say--and point-down into the bar. It even wobbles a little bit like you see in those cartoons. That shit? It's real.

The waitress falls to her knees, covering her hands.

"That won't protect you," I tell her, peering over the bar. "You're just going to get a knife in your hands."

"Ya, but it'll protect 'er 'ead," Rusty says. "So dere's dat." He takes another shot and puts the bottle politely back in place. "How much we owe ya?"

The waitress waves us off. "It's yours. Take the bottle. You earned it."

"That wasn't really the deal," I say. My face says I'm trying to make this right while I'm quietly and secretly pointing at a few bottles for Rusty to snag before we exit. "Are you sure?"

"Yes," the waitress says. "And if you brought Herman here, I swear to God, I'll kill you."

"Not if Herman does it first," Rusty says. He holds up a hand and waves goodbye. He's the first to push the doors wide open. Light pours in through the room, a bright trapezoid into the room. The air smells like car smoke and mufflers.

"Last time it was your babysitter," Rusty says. He follows me to a white Grand Am that Rusty "borrowed" the way a child borrows money from their mother's purse when she isn't looking.

"It was eighty years ago, Rus. I don't remember every detail."

"I still call bullshit."

"Say what you will. The story is true. That knife was a nice touch though."

"You liked that?" Rusty says. He sits down on the driver's side and buckles himself in. "I thought it would add a nice charm."

"And a few bottles."

He holds one up as if trying to tap it against my imaginary glass. "And a few bottles."

ABOUT THE AUTHOR

David Gearing is an educator and author of over 30 novels across multiple genres and pen names. He specializes in fiction with an LGBTQ twist and supernatural edges.

His psychology degree helps him delve deep into the anima and animus of the human mind, where he loves to stare off into the shadows. He doesn't mind when the shadows stare back.

He lives in the Pacific Northwest, but has lived all over the United States, but is mostly inspired by the Southern Gothic stories of the Deep South.

You can sign up for David's newsletter here and visit him at his website, davidgearingbooks.com, or his Publisher's website.

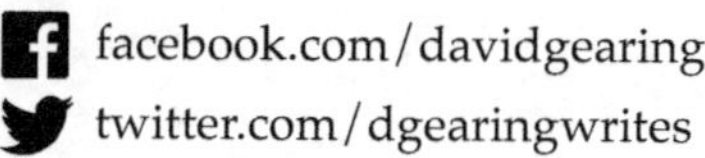

facebook.com/davidgearing
twitter.com/dgearingwrites

ALSO BY DAVID GEARING

Akusai Publishing specializes in LGBTQ centric stories, often with a supernatural edge.

Do Ya Like Dark Fantasy or Godpunk horror?

Join Hermes and Heracles in the **War of the Gods** series

Exiled from Hell (Book 1)

Reign from Heaven (Book 2)

Across the Realms (Book 3)

A Jono Grey Dark Fantasy Mystery

Apocalypse Nigh

A Flash of Silver (short story)

Give 'em A Hand (short story)

Psychological Horror

Savior

Gifted

Mad Maddy

House of Braddock

Echoes

Mr. White

Wannabe

Like Sci-Fi?

For the Republic

Reset

YA/LGBTQ

Just a Thing

Pride and Glass Unicorns

Like Thrillers?

Patient Zero

Tartarus

Bedlam

Charlie's Web Series / Thriller

The Long Game

Short Stories

Unwanted

Touched

Evaluation

Beasts

Drowning Above the Surface

Fun Fact

Eviction Day

Maria the Brave

A Shot of Neon

Writing as KD Johnson

The Shattering Series

Sword of Stone (Book 1)

Shapes of Clay (Book 2)

Halls of Shadows (Book 3)

Ray of Light (Book 4)

Man of Fire (Book 5)

Orb of Light (Book 6)

Omnibus 1: Collection of Books 1 - 3

Young Adult

Method Acting